Mrs. McNosh Hangs Up Her Wash

by Sarah Weeks
pictures by Nadine Bernard Westcott

A Laura Geringer Book
HarperFestival®
A Division of HarperCollinsPublishers

Each Monday at dawn,
Mrs. Nelly McNosh
brings out a barrel
and does a big wash.

It takes her all morning,
and when the sun's high,
she hangs what she's washed
on the clothesline to dry.

She hangs up the dresses.
She hangs up the shirts.
She hangs up the underwear,
nightgowns, and skirts.

She hangs up the stockings.
She hangs up the shoes.
She wrings out the paper
and hangs up the news.

She hangs up the dog
and his dish and his bone.
She gets a wrong number
and hangs up the phone.

She hangs up a hat,
and an old wedding gown,
and two sleepy bats,
which she hangs
upside down.

She hangs up a lamp,
and a large Christmas wreath,
and Grandpa McNosh's
removable teeth.

She hangs up a kite
by the tip of its tail.
The postman arrives,
and she hangs up the mail.

She hangs till she's hung
every last thing in sight,
including the turkey
she's roasting that night.

Each Monday by dusk,
Mrs. Nelly McNosh
has finally hung up
the last of her wash.

She takes off her apron
and lets down her hair,
then hangs herself up . . .

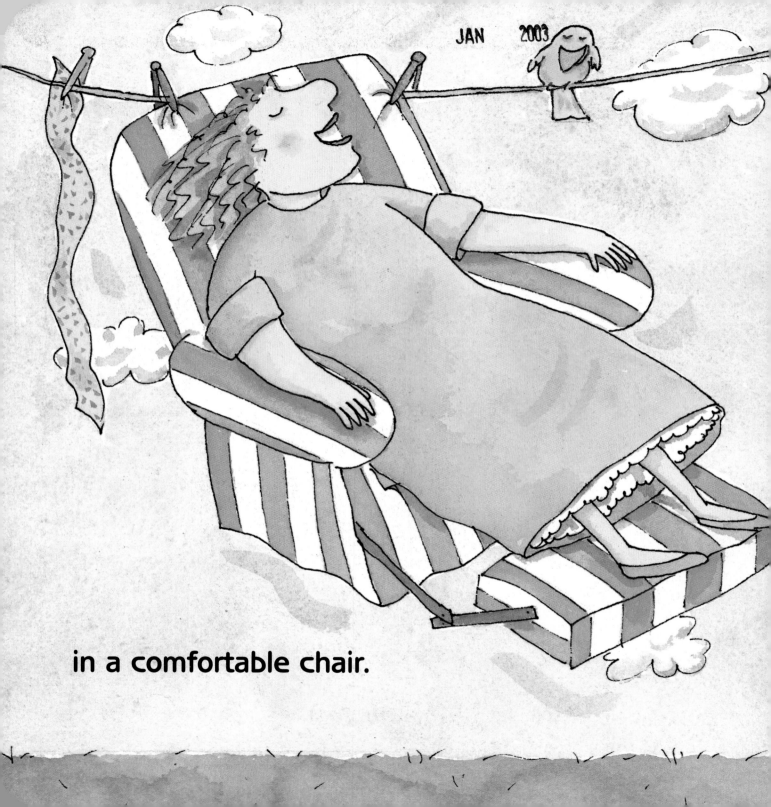

in a comfortable chair.